Charles Soule

A new travesty on Romeo and Juliet

As presented before the University club of St. Louis, January 16, 1877

A NEW TRAVESTY

ON

ROMEO AND JULIET,

As presented before the University Club of St. Louis,
January 16, 1877.

CHARACTERS:

Romeo,	Mercutio,
Juliet,	Friar Laurence,
Lord Capulet,	Nurse,
Tybalt,	Apothecary,
Chorus.	

ST. LOUIS:
G. I. JONES AND COMPANY,
1877.

PROLOGUE.

[RUMOR, *attended by* CHORUS, *discovered as the curtain rises.*]

Air—"KAFOOZALUM."

I.

RUMOR— In ancient days there lived a bard,
  A man of note, who dramas wrote;
  From all the centuries 'twere hard,
  And all the lands, to rake his peer—
  He made such perfect poetry
   That critics wink, and say they think
  Lord Bacon wrote, anonymously,
   The works of William Shak-es-peare.

CHO.— Oh! oh! Bill Shak-es-peare, Bill Shak-es-peare,
        [Bill Shak-es-peare,
  Oh! oh! Bill Shak-es-peare,
  Judge Holmes doubts your identity.

II.

RUMOR— Although his plays are very bright,
  For one who wro-te so long ago,
  Viewed in our nineteenth century light,
  His dramas no great shakes appear.
  In these fast telegraphic times,
   Some master mind we ought to find—
  Some one expert in matching rhymes,
   To modernize old Shak-es-peare.

CHO.— Oh! oh! Bill Shak-es-peare, etc.,
  You're centuries behind the times.

III.

Not to desert our race in need,
　Though modest men, we've taken pen,
And spurred our Pegasus at speed,
　In rhythmic lists to break a spear.
To-night fair Juliet's love intense,
　The wretched woe of Romeo,
With all the modern improvements,
　We reproduce from Shak-es-peare.

CHO.—　Lo! lo! Bill Shak-es-peare, etc.,
　　Re-edited at great expense.

[*Curtain.*]

ROMEO AND JULIET.

SCENE I.

A STREET IN VERONA.

[*Enter* TYBALT *and the* CAPULETS, *in campaign caps and capes, with a transparency, "For Congress! Carl Capulet!! Capulet and Reform!!!" They march in to the air, "*GALLANT 69TH.*"*]

TYB.— March on, my lads! we'll take this narrow street,
And if perchance the Montagues we meet,
Of "joint discussion" they shall have their fill.
We'll "bull-doze" 'em d. q. Aha!

CAPS.— We will!

TYB.— In this 'ere precinct we are two to one.
If any rash descendant of a gun
Dispute the figures, we will let him know
Which party runs the ward! h'm h'm?

CAPS.— Jes' so!

TYB.— As patriots we perambulate the ways
So long as pedal patriotism pays.
Our war cry is "Reform and Capulet!"
Therefore, re-form, and forward march!

CAPS.— You bet!

TYB.— But stay! methinks I apprehend a noise!
The Montagues approach! be brave, my boys.
Stand firm! don't budge—for we can surely lam 'em;
They're public pests and peculators!

CAPS.— Damn 'em!

[*Enter* MERCUTIO *and the* MONTAGUES, *also in caps and capes, with a transparency, "For Congress! Michael Montague! Montague the People's Friend!"*]

MERC.— Dress up! dress up! my stalwart men,
And guide ye by the right!
Else will the villain Capulets
Assert ye to be tight.

A patriot's fire doth us inspire,
We'll march both fast and far,
For, when we to our hall retire,
   A lunch awaits!
MONTS.—   Aha!
MERC.— In this parade we seek no aid
From meretricious drum;
We only wish our thirst allayed
With good old "Rye."
MONTS.—   *Yum, yum!*
MERC.— Then, comrades dear, one rousing cheer
For Montague essay,
Free speech, free press, free lunch, free beer!
Now then, hip! hip!
MONTS. [*very faintly*]—   Hooray!
MERC.— Aha! the Capulets! the hour has come!
Avaunt, base wretches! rag-tag! bob-tail! scum!
TYB.— What, *scum?* Has't come to this extreme?
Up guards and at 'em! let the eagle scream!!
CAPS.—   Ha!
MONTS.—   Ha!!
CAPS.—   Ha!!!
MONTS.—   Ha!!!!
MERC.— Before we fight, brave sons of warlike pas,
Suppose we raise a battle hymn to Mars?
TYB.— Not we! If you intend sincerely to attack us,
We'll call upon a deity who'll Back-us.
CAPS.— Oh! oh! Bacchus!
MONTS.—   Oh! oh! Bacchus!

[*Each man draws a flask.*]

MONTS.— Let's take a whiff of whisky!
CAPS.—   Drink it down!
MONTS.— Let's take a whiff of whisky!
                    Drink it down!
ALL—   Let's take a whiff of whisky,
It will make us fighting frisky!   [down.
Drink it down, drink it down, drink it down, down,
Down it trickles, trickles, down it trickles, trickles,
Down it trickles into our very boots!
CAPS.— Oh, take another nip,
MONTS.—   Drink it down!

Caps.— Oh, take another nip,

Monts.—   Drink it down!

All.— Oh, take another nip, and may the best man whip!
Drink it down, drink it down, drink it down,
                    [down, down.
Down it gurgles, etc.

Merc.— Attention! company! and action front!
I'll seek a post where I can bear the brunt.

[Retires to the flies.]

Tyb.— Advance, my gallant soldiers! strike the foe!
If needed, I will be—six squares below.

[Retires.]

Merc. [*peeps out*]—
Now for the combat! on ye brave!
Who rush to glory or the grave!

Tyb. [*peeps out*]—
Come one, come all, this rock shall fly
From its firm base as soon as I.

[Montagues *and* Capulets *fight to music. Enter* Capulet *briskly.*]
Air—"Stop, Boys, Stop."

Cap. [*sings*]—
Stop, boys! stop your little fighting,
Rioting like this has no excuse.
You must stop your little row,
It's a thing I can't allow,
And I tell you that I own the calaboose.
[*speaks*]—
Why all this fratricidal fray and fuss?
Tybalt! Mercutio! why should this be thus?
If such disorders should be common, why, sirs,
I must apply for federal supervisors!
Such shocking rows and rumpuses as this yer
Will justify my mustering the militia!
I hereby read the riot act (in verse),
And give you just—a fortnight—to disperse.
If still found fighting when that period's o'er,
We will,—well, read the riot act once more.
Arouse us at your peril! So, beware!
Yours truly, Capulet, Esquire, Lord Mayor!

Tyd.— Pardon us, sire! Your righteous ire
We deprecate, and agree to retire,
I and the friar, our corps entire;
Will put up our swords, and speedily hie a-
Way to enquire what penance dire
Conduct like ours would best require;
And if any liar should foully aspire
To say I am not a thorough complier
With all that your Honor may ever desire.
I promise to hire a funeral pyre,
And cremate the ass in the hottest of fire:
Till he leave this mire, to go up higher,
And takes his place in the angelic choir,
And—

[*All stop their ears.*]

Cap.— Stop! Stop, young man! Of such prolific stuff
Two dozen lines are more than quantum suff!
What say you, friends, will you preserve the peace,
Or shall I call a section of police?
I pray ye, grant me this one little boon,
   And promise not to get upon another tear:
If so, I'll ask you into yon saloon—
   Will ye swear to break the peace no more?
All—   *We swear!*

Air—"Soldiers' Chorus," *from Faust.*

Cho.— No, sir, we never will fight any more,
No, sir, we never will fight any more,
No, sir, we never will fight any more,   [any more.
Never will fight, never will fight, never will fight
Solo— If you will treat whenever we meet,
We never will kick up a fuss in the street;
If you will treat whenever we meet—
   You bet your life.
Beer's better than bickering;
Whisky and sugar's about the thing:
Here's hoping you'll often bring
Us free toddy and sling.
Cho.— No, sir, etc.
Tyb.— If I correctly understood you, you alluded
To some saloon; or, if you didn't, who did?

CAP.--   'Twas I, sir; I shall be profoundly proud
        To walk across with you and treat the crowd.

           Air—"COME, OH, COME WITH ME."

CAP.—   Come, oh, come with me,
          The tapster is waiting,
        Come, oh, come with me,
          The bottle's rotating,
        Come, oh, come with me,
          My bidding is free,
        And we will indulge in—
          A cup of iced tea.
        And do not pray be backward,
          'Tis well understood
        That Hellery will trust me—
          My credit is good.

ALL—   Come, oh, come with him,
          The tapster is waiting :
        Come, oh come with him,
          The bottle's rotating ;
        Come, oh, come with him,
          His bidding is free,
        And we will indulge in—
          A cup of iced tea.

           [*Exeunt all but* MERCUTIO.]

MERC.—   And now my followers are safely caged
        Where they'll remain until the day is aged,
        Hobnobbing with their ancient enemies,
        I'll take a little time to tend to biz.
        These politics !—these beastly politics—
        They get a fellow in a fearful fix,
        Just think of marching round a crowd like that
        In such a cape as this—and such a hat !
        Yet 'tis the only way a man can thrust his
        Claim to a place as coroner or justice.
        This tedious round of marching and display
        Is high ambition's only modern way.
        Who comes ?—I hope he does not know me—oh !

           [*Enter* ROMEO.]

        'Tis but my love-lorn kinsman Romeo.
        Why, howdy, Romy ! what do you bring for news ?

ROM.—   Dearest Mercutio, I have got the blues!

Duet. Air—"Long, Long Ago."

Rom. *and* Merc.—

I am / He is the hero of this little tale,

I'm / He's Romeo, I'm / he's Romeo.

I am / He is that sadly susceptible male,

I'm / He's Romeo, Romeo.

No other lover has e'er done what I did ;
For when my / his girl to eternity glided,

I / He bought some poison and just suicided.

Rash Romeo, Romeo !
Please get your handkerchiefs ready for use.

I'm / He's Romeo, I'm / he's Romeo ;

Sighs shall come copious, groans grow profuse,

I'm / He's Romeo, Romeo ;

For when you learn the depth of my / his woes,

Tears will go weltering down every nose ;
You'll *shriek* with a chorus of " ahs " and of " ohs,"
Poor Romeo, Romeo !

Merc.— Well, Romeo ! who has caused these blues of thine ?
Rom.— The fair, the chaste, the unexpensive Rosaline.
Merc.— Unexpressive, Shakespeare has't in *As you Like It*.
Rom.— Unexpensive is my word, and I exactly strike it.
My other flames have cost me heaps of cash.
Whenever I have felt a former " smash,"
I've been obliged to send the girl bouquets,
And pamper her in many costly ways—
Candy and gloves, and jewelry and sich,
   To take her to the opera in a carriage,
To court exactly as if I were rich,
   And not dependent for my grub on marriage !
Why ! when I loved the beauteous Sophia.
Merc. [*aside*]—
   'Tis but a week since he was swearing by her.

Rom.— I kept a memorandum of my follies,—
What think you the sum total of the whole is?
During the thirteen days the fever lasted,
I opera-ed and present-ed and repast-ed
That loveliest of Verona's lovely daughters
Just ninety-seven dollars and three-quarters!
Now Rosaline's content with mere devotion.
If her admirer testifies emotion
By keeping up a constant battery
Of sighs, and prayers, and fervid flattery,
She needs no presents—hasn't a desire
But just to sit and listen by the fire.
And so I push my courtship—whose expense,
Thus far, has been six car-fares—thirty cents.

Merc.— Oh, you'll get tired of her within a week,
And find some fairer face and fresher freak.

Rom.— No, never! 'Tis my last and truest love;
I swear it, by this dainty little glove!

Merc.— We'll see, my fickle friend! What, ho! A sail!
It scuttles down before a rattling gale!

[*Enter* Nurse, *running, followed by* Apothecary.]

Air—"Little Brown Jug."

Nurse— Gentle strangers, rescue me
From this impudent rowdee!
He spoke to me upon the street—
A man I ne'er before did meet.

Rom. *and* Merc.—
Ha! ha! ha! who can it be?
It is the old apothecaree! ·
Ha! ha! ha! whom do we see?
It is the old apothecaree!

Nurse— I told him plain to go away—
He begged and prayed I'd let him stay;
I up and slapped his ugly face,
Then ran away and he gave chase.

Rom. *and* Merc.—
Ha! ha! ha! etc.

Nurse— I beg of you, good gentlemen,
Don't let him speak to me again;
For if he can't leave me in peace,
I'll give him up to the police.

Rom. *and* Merc.—
   Ha! ha! ha! etc.
Merc.— What! pill-compounder, has it come to this?
   Art *thou* accused of little gallantries?
   And yet, thy choice becomes thee not so ill—
   A college boy would call this lass a pill!
   But stay! If I recall aright the play,
   Shakespeare locates you off in Mantua,
   And doesn't introduce you, even there,
   Until the fifth act. How, sir, can you dare
   Intrude upon us in our opening scene?
Apoth.—Mercutio, it's abominably mean
   For you and Romeo to want all the fun,
   And give us far more gifted actors none.
   You can't come that on me; I claim the right
   To play a leading character to-night.
   If you don't like it—lump it! Shakespeare's dead,
   With his ideas we're playing merry Ned.
Merc.— Well, be it so! If Romeo don't stickle
   Upon his rights—I do not care a nickel.
   But tell us who this woman is, and why
   You woo an unwilling lass so zealously?
Apoth.—May't please your worships, I did idly wander,
   When I espied the lovely damsel yonder;
   I saw, I loved—I tried to tell her so—
   I claim as good a right, I'd have you know,
   To sudden love affairs, as Romeo!
   Sweet vision! loveliest female in Verona,
   I only seek to be thy lawful owner! [quest:
Rom.— Why, ma'am, you surely can't find fault with you
   Of this good druggist we have made a conquest.
Nurse— Indeed! If so it be that he's sincere,
   I'll not be angry, though it seems so queer!
   But can you tell me, sirs, where I can see
   The gallant Tybalt and his company?
Merc.— I saw them here anon. In soothing rhythm
   I would enquire what business you have with 'em?
Nurse— My master, Capulet, (whom you know, I ween,)
   Altho' he's awful rich, is awful mean,
   He keeps no servants, only me, the nurse,
   (And don't give me no decent wages, scarce;)
   He makes me do the work of half a score—

I cooks, and makes the beds, and tends the door,
I dresses Missis, and her daughter Jule,
(A peart, and proud, and pretty little fool,)
I does the arrants, as I'm doin' now ;
I 've run a dozen miles, I vum and vow,
Until I'm out of breath and out of patience
A-worrying with his dratted invitations.

MERC.— He gives a hop ?

NURSE— To-night—a reg'lar blow out !

[*Exeunt* NURSE *and* APOTHECARY.]

MERC.— Thank you—my friend and I but rarely go out,
But since you ask us, we will both be there.

ROM.— Tut! tut! Mercutio !

MERC.— This is my affair—
'Twill be a h. o. t. and we'll go to't.

ROM.— But 'tisn't proper, and my party suit
Is threadbare and all stained with ice and fruit.

MERC.— Never you mind—just trust yourself to me,
This Capulet's fair daughter you must see ;
She's pretty as a peach ; she'll take the shine
Quite off your unexpensive Rosaline.

ROM.— I do protest !

MERC.— She's not a girl to buck at ;
I tell you she will have her little ducat !

ROM.— How so ?

MERC.— The firm of Capulet and O'Rourke
Made mints of money—

ROM.— In what line ?

MERC.— In pork.
He realized when pork was at its fattiest,
And now a blamed aristocrat he *ist*.

ROM.— Enough ! to see the maid I fairly yearn.
Lead on ! sir !

MERC.— Hush ! the roysterers return.

[*Enter* MONTAGUES *and* CAPULETS.]

Air—"BOWLING GREEN."

CHO.— We Caps and Monts, we had a fight,
We fit all day and we fit all night ;
Old Cap came and made us stop,
And treated us to ginger-pop.

Bully for the old fellow-ow-ow,
Bully for the old fellow,
Old Cap came and made us stop,
And treated us to ginger-pop ;

A better feeling we've effected,
Don't care a copper who's elected,
Except that we will vote and bet
For jolly old Judge Capulet.

Bully for the old follow-ow-ow, etc.

[*Curtain.*]

SCENE II.

[Garden before CAPULET'S *house. Balconies right and left.* GUESTS *assembled.]*

Air—" MERMAID."

I.

CHO.— Oh, here we are, all ready for the fun,
    We're bound for a high old spree;
Oh, here we are, all ready for the fun,
    Whatever it may be;
For the light fantastic toe,
Or the spirits fluid flow.   [we bring,
We will dance or we will sing, and good apertures
All the supper we can find away to stow-ow-ow,
All the supper we can find away to stow.

II.

                  [feed,
Then trot out your host, and your fiddles and your
And begin this little party right away!   [feed,
Then trot out your host, and your fiddles and your
And do not keep us waiting till we're gray;
And be sure you don't forget
Our whistles and our throats to wet,
For we're generally allowed to be a dry old crowd
Wherever we are known, Capulet-let-let,
Wherever we are known, Capulet.

[Enter CAPULET.]

CAP.— Welcome, my friends, to this sequestered spot,
'Tis but a modest, unpretending cot;
My means, you know, are narrow,
GUESTS [*aside*]—   What a whopper!
CAP.— But with my friends I'd share my latest copper.
These small impromptu hospitalities
Are my delight; and this occasion is,
Of all, the most delightful; for I see

Around me all the youth and chivalry
Of proud Verona. Welcome! once again.

[*Enter* Apothecary.]

Apoth. [*aside*]—

    I found at last a dry and roomy drain,
    And crept beneath the garden wall; once here,
    In such a motley mob, I do not fear
    Detection; being *in*, they cannot find me *out* ;
    I'll boldly join the crowd and look about,
    Until I find my beauteous and bewitching
    Young goddess of the nursery and kitching.

Cap.—   Nurse! nurse!

Apoth.—   He calls her name.

Cap.—   Oh, nurse!

[*Enter* Nurse.]

Nurse—   Sir'ee!
    I'm coming!

Apoth.—   Ah, she comes! 'tis she! 'tis she!
    Extract of sweetness!

Nurse—   Gracious, let me be!
    My master calls!

Apoth.—   Grant me one little word,
    And say thou lov'st me!

Nurse—   Don't be so absurd!
    Wait till I've waited on——

Cap.—   Where are you, nurse?
    Odds bodkins! Zounds! Dog-gone it!

Nurse—   Hear him curse!
    Here, sir! what's wanted?

Cap.—   When you're called, come quicker!

Nurse— Goodness gracious me, the man's in liquor!

Cap.—   You go and say to Mrs. Capulet,
    We want her here to lead the opening set.

[*Exit* Nurse. *Enter* Romeo *and* Mercutio.]

Air—"Crambambuli."

Rom. *and* Merc. [*to the guests*]—

    We trust you won't betray,
      Good friends, our little secret ;
    We've come to-night without invite,
      And here we mean to stay.

GUESTS.—You've come to-night without invite,
    To tell on you would not be right,
      We'll not your trust betray,
      We'll not your trust betray.

ROM. *and* MERC.—
    Don't tell old Capulet,
     'Twould spoil our undertaking;
    And such a freak takes so much cheek,
     It ought success to get.

GUESTS.—Yes! such a freak takes so much cheek,
    We'll never let your secret leak,
      Nor tell old Capulet,
      Nor tell old Capulet.

          [*Enter* NURSE.]

CAP.—   Well, where is Mrs. C.?
NURSE—   She won't come down!
CAP.—   Will not come down? And why, I'd like to know?
NURSE— She says your company's a noisy, low,
    Intemperate set of pot-house politicians—
    She'll not come nowhere near 'em.
CAP.—   Great Omniscience,
    What awful ills connubial bliss is heir to!
    I'd like to drag her down, but do not dare to;
    Fetch Juliet, she'll not turn up her nose
    At any sort of practicable beaux.

          [*Exit* NURSE.]

MERC.— There, Romeo, you see what brass will do—
    Now we are here, let's see the party through.
    Suppose we get an introduction to our host?
ROM.—   Is *that* the kind of impudence you boast?
    Let's not put any friend to such a bother—
    We'll just waltz in and introduce each other.
    Judge Capulet, pray let me introduce you
    To my distinguished friend, Major Mercutio.
CAP.—   I'm highly honored.
MERC.   Now you know *me*, you
    Should likewise know the gallant Colonel Romeo.
    Let me present him.
CAP.—   Sir, your most obedient.
ROM.—   Well, Cushe, what do you think of my expedient?

          [*They retire.*]

CAP.— All right, I s'pose! Here, Tybalt, who in thunder
Are those two gay young fellows over yonder?
TYB.— Methinks I've seen their faces somewhere, sire;
I'll take the first occasion to enquire.

[*Enter* NURSE *and* JULIET.]

Air—" EVER BE HAPPY."

I.

CHO.— Hail to the fairest of all Verona's fair,
Hail to our pride and pet!
Sweeter than the sweetest, bright beyond compare,
Lovely little Juliet!
Eyes all admire thee, hearts all desire thee,
Universal worship thy loveliness compels;
Sweeter than the sweetest, bright beyond compare,
Best of Verona's belles!

II.

Hail to the greatest of all our heiresses,
Sure of a million net,
Richer than the richest, with solid charms to bless,
Golden little Juliet!
Younger sons bespeak thee, empty pockets seek
thee,
Universal longing thy affluence impels,
Richer than the richest, with solid charms to bless,
Best of Verona's belles!

CAP.— My Juliet, gentlemen, my only che-ild!
She's just fourteen to-day—
NURSE [*aside*]— Oh, draw it mild!
She's nearly thirty-four, or forty, may be!
CAP.— My tender dove,(stand straight, you jade!) my baby,
Embrace me, sweetest! (mind, you little devil!
If I detect you flirting at this revel,
I'll lock you up a week on bread and water.)
Now, Tybalt, lead the dancing with my daughter.
Take partners, gentlemen, and form a set;
We'll blunder through an opening minuet.

[TYBALT *approaches to take* JULIET, *but* ROMEO *cuts in before him.* APOTHECARY *leads out the* NURSE, *and dancing commences. Minuet: Air as in* "DON GIOVANNI;" *words every alternate line.*]

    *   *   *   *   *

MERC.— We need more belles and fewer beaux—

    *   *   *   *   *

NURSE— You're stepping on my toes—

    *   *   *   *   *

CAP.— This dance I do not understand—

    *   *   *   *   *

JULIET— Do not squeeze my hand—

Air changes to "HIGGINS'S COTERIE."

JUL.— Change the figure into a jigger—
Strike a tune that has some vigor;
This walk-around of a minuet
Won't answer for this set.

CHO.— Join hands and form a line;
Step out with fire and fling;
March down the stage—ah! isn't this fine—
But it's mighty hard to sing.   [death,
But while we have any breath, we'll all be in at the
And it's mighty lively dancing at Capulet's coterie.

APOTH. [*mopping his brow*]—
This dancing may be fun for some, but I
Prefer to take such fun vicariously.
My friend, what time o' night in these gay upper
Circles do they propose to trot out supper?

MERC.— About eleven Capulet feeds his guests;
His feeding, tho', is never food for jests.

APOTH.—Why, Capulet's rich, he ought to gorge us well.

MERC.— Yes, rich, but mean; his supper is a sell—
Hark what he says:

CAP.—   Now, friends, I rather guess you
Are warm and tired with dancing; to refresh you,
I have a little foolish banquet toward.
Fall to anon!

APOTH.—   What says the ancient blowhard?

MERC.— He says fall to—go in, old chap, and try it!
I cannot stand the Dio Lewis diet!

Air—"ROBIN ADAIR."

MERC.— What have we here to eat?

ROM.—   Bread in this dish!

MERC.— Ain't that a plate of meat?
ROM.—   Only salt fish!
ALL—   Is this all we're to get?
        Stingy old fraud, Capulet!
        What a vile spread to set!
        Bread and salt fish!

MERC.— What's in that jug to drink?
ROM.—   Beer, by its looks!
MERC.— There is champagne, we think?
ROM.—   Only Ike Cook's.
ALL—   Is this all we're to get?
        Stingy old fraud, Capulet!
        What a vile spread to set!
        Beer and Ike Cook's.

APOTH.—Well, boys, this is a mighty light and scarce tea;
        I don't feel hungry, but I'm very thirsty.
        Let's sample Cappy's beer, and when we're beery
        We'll try to get away with his Imperial.   [all,
        Here's at you, Judge!
CAP.—   I thank you, sir! drink hearty!
        Who is that old disreputable party?
        It seems to me there's lots of strangers here!
        He has a powerful exhaust on beer!
        Pray can I serve you, sir, with something more?
TYB.—   Uncle, I've found him out! I thirst for gore!
CAP.—   Why, what's the matter?
TYB.—   Yonder gay young fool,
        Who's making love so openly to Jule,
        Is Romeo, the heir of Montague!
CAP.—   Aha! my rival's son? It can't be true!
TYB.—   It is! I'll face the villain and denounce him!
CAP.—   Softly, good nephew, he's my guest!
TYB.—   I'll bounce him!
CAP.—   No, no, not now! Fill, gallant gentlemen!
        Your healths!
TYB.—   Oh, let me at him!
CAP.—   Once again!
        (Peace! Tybalt!) pray you fill your glasses high!
        (I will not have it!) Jove! but they are dry!

[MERCUTIO, ROMEO, JULIET, and GUESTS, come forward. CAPULET and
                TYBALT remain in rear.]

MERC. [*aside to Romeo*]—
>That's it, my boy, I'm watching you, go in !
>Direct assault is always sure to win.
>[*to Juliet*]—
>It strikes us all, my dear Miss Capulet,
>That you're a cool and consummate coquette.

Air—Adapted from the "GRANDE DUCHESSE."

JUL.— You err when you call Juliet,

ALL.— Juliet !

JUL.— In the slightest degree a coquette.

ALL.— Coquette.

JUL.— I will boldly assert I am less of a flirt
>Than any one here ever met.
>And yet, if I e'er took a beau,
>I'd fancy your friend Romeo—Romeo !

CHO.— Romeo, Romeo,
>She 'd fancy the dashing Romeo, you know ;
>Romeo, Romeo,
>She 'd fancy our friend Romeo.

CAP.— (Tybalt, you hush !) They 're getting set up, surely.
>I must break up the party prematurely.   [go to ?
>What—nurse ! Oh, nurse ! Where did the old fool
>Why, bless my soul, the nurse has got a beau, too !
>And Juliet—I sadly fear that she's hit !

TYB.— I'll drink his blood !

CAP.— Oh, drink some beer, and cheese it !
>Come, Jule !

JUL.— My father calls me, I must go !
>Farewell, adieu, ta-ta, sweet Romeo !

ROM.— Adieu but for an hour—ere you have laid you
>Adown to sleep, I'll come to serenade you.
>My sun is set !—I'll go to Faust's and take
>An oyster stew, to keep myself awake.

[*Exit.*]

CAP.— Friends, I should like another waltz or redowa,
>But it is somewhat past our usual bed hour.
>I do not wish to hint, but still, you know,
>I really think 'tis time for you to go.

MERC.— No, no, old chap, you can't come that on us !
>We've just begun to get hilarious.

You go to bed, and take the girls away ;
We frankly tell you we propose to stay !
Good-night, old boy !

CAP.—   Old boy ! and I a judge !
Juliet, leave the drunken fools and trudge ;
With boozy sleep their revels soon will end off.

[*Exeunt* CAPULET, JULIET, *and* NURSE.]

MERC.— Say, boys, let's give the girls a proper send off!

Air—"GOOD-NIGHT, LADIES."

CHO.—   Good-night [*hic*], ladies !
        Good-night [*hic*], ladies !
        Good-night [*hic*], ladies,
     'F you're goin' to leave us [*hic*].
Sorry to see you've got to go, got to go, got to go,
Sorry to see you've got to go,
    Got to go to bed.
Sorry to see you've got to go, got to go, got to go,
Sorry to see you've got to go,   •
    Got to go to bed.

MERC.— I shay, old feller [*hic*], I feel shleepy, too !
APOTH.—Jes' sho ! what [*hic*] you 'bserve is toorooly true,
Letsh take anozzer zrink and shing a shong :
Wha'sh that about we won't go home till mo'n'g?

CHO.— We won't [*hic*] go home till morning, etc.

[*At end of chorus all stagger and fall symmetrically,* APOTHECARY *at back, others at sides, with legs projecting. In this position they sing the refrain more and more faintly, finally ending off in a snore.*]

[*Curtain.*]

SCENE III.

[Before the curtain rises the following chorus is heard :]

Air—"Pull Down the Blinds."

Cho.— Turn down the gas, turn down the gas,
'Tis night in Verona, turn down the gas !
Turn down the gas, turn down the gas;
Simulate darkness and turn down the gas.

[Curtain rises. Capulet's garden. Apothecary lying at back of stage. Guests' legs projecting at sides. Cats and dogs are heard.]

"Dream Chorus" of Sleepers. *Air*—"Du, Du Liegst Mir Im Herzen."

[*Snore, snore,*] we lie uneasy,
[*Snore, snore,*] in our cold beds ;
[*Snore, snore,*] 'tis growing freezy,
We shall get colds in our heads,
[*Snore, snore, snore, snore,*]
We shall get colds in our heads,
[*Snore, snore, snore, snore,*]
We shall get colds in our heads.

[Enter Romeo.]

Rom.— Confound these logs ! The man that does the chores
Has left old Capulet's wood-pile out o' doors.

[Snores heard.]

Great Scott ! how loud fair Juliet's father snores !
If I can hear him here, outside, so plain,
Poor Mrs. C., within, must get profane ;
But p'r'aps she snores as well. Yes ! I detect
A second snore, of feminine effect ;
A second ? aye, a third ! can it be she ? Ah !
No ! I reprobate the vile idea—
A Juliet could not snore.

[Stumbles over Apothecary.]

By Jove ! I can't turn
Without a trip ! I wish I'd brought a lantern.
This is the house ; I wonder whether that is
The gentle Juliet's balcony and lattice ? [*Whistles.*]

[*The* APOTHECARY *sits up and rubs his eyes.*]　　[yawn!

APOTH.—"Wo won't go home till morning!" S'cuse my
　Tight? Yes, sir, and asleep on Capulet's lawn.
　One more of Fortune's singular reverses!
　I wonder where my pretty little nurse is.
　Now if I only had a way to know it. her
　Chamber must be near here—I'll reconnoitre.

[JULIET *appears on balcony.*]

ROM.— 　She comes! I feel as if all Heaven had sprung a leak!
　　Oh, would I were a number eight and three-quarters
　　　　　upon that hand, that I might touch that cheek!
JUL.— 　Who whistles?
ROM.— 　　　　　Romeo, thy slave! What's that?
JUL.— 　'Tis but the harmless necessary cat,
　　(As Shakspeare says) the dog that bays the moon:
　　With our new love all nature seems in tune.
　　The animals who, inharmonious,
　　Shriek their affection, sympathize with us.

Air—" BULL-DOG."

JUL.— 　Oh, the bull-dog in the yard,
ROM.— 　　And the tomcat on the roof;
JUL.— 　Oh, the bull-dog in the yard,
ROM.— 　　And the tomcat on the roof.
DUET— 　Oh, the bull-dog in the yard,
　　And the tomcat on the roof,
　　Are practicing the Highland fling,
　　And singing opera bouffe.
CHO.— 　Barking bow, wow, wow, wow, wow, wow, wow,
　　Mewing miaow, yow, yow, yow, yow, yow, yow,
　　Barking bow, wow, wow, wow, wow,
　　Mewing miaow, yow, yow, yow, yow,
　　Bow, wow, wow—miaow, yow, yow,
　　Bow, miaow, wow!
JUL.— 　Says the tomcat to the dog,
ROM.— 　　Oh, set your ears agog,
JUL.— 　Says the tomcat to the dog,
ROM.— 　　Oh, set your ears agog,
DUET— 　Says the tomcat to the dog,
　　Oh, set your ears agog,
　　For Jule's about to tête-à-tête
　　With Romeo, incog.

[*Chorus as before.*]

JUL.—   Says the bull-dog to the cat,
ROM.—   What do you think they're at?
JUL.—   Says the bull-dog to the cat,
ROM.—   What do you think they're at?
DUET.—   Says the bull-dog to the cat,
         What do you think they're at?
         They're spooning in the dead of night,
         And where's the harm in that?
CHO.—   Barking bow, wow, etc.

[NURSE *appears at window, back.*]

NURSE— What's all this row?
APOTH.—   Oh, hush! my sweet, 'tis I,
       Thy fond and faithful Apo-the-ca-ry!
JUL.— Oh, Romeo, Romeo, wherefore art thou Romeo?
ROM.— Ill-timed conundrums why propound unto me? Oh,
       I give it up!
NURSE—   You drunken drug-concocter, quit!
       Don't fool around here; but just git up and git.
JUL.— I love thee, Romeo! Wilt thou marry me?
ROM.— I'd like to, but our politics don't agree.
     UL.— That's immaterial; I do not care
       A copper who is President or Mayor—
       I only want a husband.
APOTH.—   Lovely creature,
       I wish my lips were long enough to reach your
       Too distant window!
NURSE—   Well, as it appears
       Your lips won't reach, why don't you try your ears?
ROM.— My darling, let me make one brief enquiry—
       If I mistake not your respected sire, he
       Won't give you any cash in hand, unless
       You marry as he wishes.
JUL.—   Romeo, I possess
       Two hundred thousand in my proper right.
ROM.— Heart of my heart, I'll marry thee to-night!
APOTH.—Sweet spirit, hear my prayer!
NURSE—   Your drunken tone
       Shows you should let sweet spirits, sir, alone!
JUL.— No, not to-night—to-morrow will I go

To Friar Laurence, and be Mrs. Romeo.
And dost thou love me?

ROM.—   · Yes, by yodder bood. [*Sneezes.*],

JUL.—   Oh, swear dot by the bood, the ideodstadt
bood. [*Sneezes.*]

APOTH.—By bodel of all lovelidess, I wish you
Would sbile upod by love—oh, ackersnish-oo !

[SLEEPERS *rouse, sit up, and sing softly to the air,* "MARCHING THRO'
GEORGIA."]

MERC.—   Seems to me I hear a noise,
Theres some one talking near ;
Let us through the midnight gloom
Diligently peer,
To find what dang'rous characters.
Are loitering round here,
Under the cover of the darkness.

CHO. [*softly*]— Hullo ! Hullo !
We think we apprehend,
Hullo ! Hullo !
A case of "Mutual Friend,"
Two souls with but a single thought,
Two hearts as one that blend,
Under the cover of the darkness.

[*They rise and gather at back of stage.*]

MERC.—   Wonder what it's best to do ?
Should we interfere ?
No, it's not our funeral,
That is very clear !
But we ought to let them know
We can overhear,
Under the cover of the darkness.

[*They come forward and shout.*]

CHO.--   Hullo ! Hullo !
We think we apprehend, etc.

ROM.— We are discovered ! Fiends and furies snatch me !

JUL.—   I'd faint, if Romeo were up here to catch me !

ROM.—   Good friends, do not betray us !

CAP. [*within*]—   What's that rumpus ?

JUL.—   My father !

Rom.—   Now do the fates us sure encompass !
Oh, shield our secret !

[*Cats.*]

Cap. [*within*]—   This is too appalling !
Give me a boot-jack ! stop your caterwauling !
Rom.—   Devise some fib to tell him if he comes,
Some lie of lies, some hummiest of hums !

[*Cats.*]

Merc.—   We'll say the cats aroused us and we chased 'em !
Cap. [*within*]—
Now, Mrs. Capulet, just see me paste 'em !

[*Appears on balcony with boot-jack and candle. Tableau. Lights.*]

Air—" Litoria.*"*

Cap.—   Why Juliet, how came you here ?
Jul.—   I came to chase those cats !
Cap.—   Romeo, why do you appear ?
Rom.—   To hunt those blasted cats !
Cap.—   You, gentlemen, why haunt my house ?
Guests—   Because your cats have haunted us !
Cap.—   I thought you'd finished your carouse.
Guests—   We came back after cats !
Cho.—   We've chased them here, we've chased them there,
We've found at last their hidden lair,
We tear and swear, but they don't care.
Hang the rascals ! Scat ! !
Cap.—   You talked to him, unless I err.
Jul.—   I only spoke to cats !
Cap.—   And wer'n't you making love to her ?
Rom.—   Oh, no—I courted cats.
Cap.—   I thought I heard you try to sing.
Guests—   'Twas cat-calls we were uttering.
Cap.—   All right, we'll all join in and fling
All.—   Missiles at the cats.
Cho.—   We've chased them here, etc.

[*Curtain.*]

SCENE IV.

FRIAR LAURENCE'S *cell; bare walls—no furniture.* FRIAR LAURENCE
and chorus of FRIARS.

Air—" LAST CIGAR," (*" Dearest May."*)

FR. LA.—Good-morning, gents, I'm glad to see
    A good array of friars ;
    Unusual solemnity
    This nuptial job requires.
    The pair we are about to splice
    Are genuine F. F. V.'s.
    We ought to get a handsome price—
    Are you prepared to please ?

CHO. *of* FRIARS—
    Oh, yes, we're here arrayed,
    In neat and nobby dress ;
    All due responses shall be made
    With sweet sonorousness.
        [Repeat.]

FR. LA.—I very much regret, my reverend cronies,
    The private nature of these ceremonies;
    So large a corps of clergymen would grace
    A stylish wedding in a swellier place.
    To match our turn-out, we should have, say, eight
    Superbly lovely bridesmaids; half a score
    Of gorgeous ushers posing 'round the door ;
    A bang-up banquet ; floods of food, to wit:
    Oysters and salads—

FRIARS—   Don't allude to it.

FR. LA.—I won't, if it disturbs the pious quiet
    Engendered by our plain monastic diet.
    Listen ! methinks I can detect, my hearties,
    The footsteps of the high contracting parties.

        [Knocking right.]

        Air—" DOODAH."

FR. LA.—   Some one's knocking at the door,
FRIARS—   Who's there ? Who's there ?

FR. LA.—   Some one's knocking at the door,
FRIARS—   Who's there ?
ROM. [*outside*]—   Romeo ?
ALL—   Here comes young Montague
        To wed his dearest foe—
        Come in, sir, we're ready for to put you through—
        Enter Romeo !

[*Enter* ROMEO *right.*]

FR. LA.—Good-morning, sir; aren't you a little laggard ?
ROM.—   No, sir! I'm sure I'm right—I time by Jaccard.
FR. LA.—'Tis well—I would not for the world the fact doubt ;
        One thing is plain—the *bridegroom* has'nt backed
                                            [out.
[*Knocking left.*]

FR. LA.—   Some one's knocking at the door,
FRIARS—   Who's there ? Who's there ?
FR. LA.—   Some one's knocking at the door,
                            Who's there ?
JUL. [*outside*]—   Juliet.
ALL—   And here's the blushing bride,
        The sweet Miss Capulet ;
        Come in—he's here, all ready to be tied—
        Enter Juliet !

[*Enter* JULIET *left.*]

FR. LA.—Welcome, sweet child! Aren't you a trifle late ?
JUL.—   Perhaps—my watch has stopped, I grieve to state.
FR. LA.—No woman ever thinks her watch to wind—
        I'm glad to see *you* haven't changed your mind.
        Well, are you ready, children, for beginning?
        If so, we'll commence the needful chinning.
JUL.—   Go on, good father !
ROM.—   Yes, pitch in !
FR. LA.—   Yet stay !
        Who gives this lovely damosel away ?
        Where are your witnesses ? We can't progress
        Without the usual appurtenances.
ROM.—   I clean forgot ! What shall we do about 'em ?
JUL.—   Can't we be married just as well without 'em ?
FR. LA.—Of course not. 'Twouldn't be one-half a show ;

Would it, my ghostly coadjutors?

FRS.— No!

[Knocking heard right and left.]

JUL.— My father!

ROM.— Just my blasted luck! I'll bet
It *is* the old paternal Capulet.

JUL.— Oh, hide me, reverend friar!

FR. LA.— Hide you? Oh, hang!
There's not a cupboard in my whole shebang.
You see it all—there's no place here to hide.
They're knocking—don't you hear?—on either side.
I have it! Lucky sacerdotal features [ers.
Are these long skirts—we'll hide behind the preach-

*[ROMEO and JULIET hide each behind a FRIAR. FRIAR LAURENCE goes
to door right.]*

FR. LA.—Come in!

[Enter NURSE.]

NURSE— Now, Parson Laurence, this is shocking,
To keep parishioners so long a knocking.
Excuse, your reverences, my imperence,
I see you're holding district conference—
I've come to find Miss Juliet, who took
Herself away, while I was acting cook,
Down the back alley, but I chanced to see her,
And up and followed; she is somewhere here.

[Violent knocking left.]

FR. LA.—Come in, come in, thou most persistent pounder!

[Enter APOTHECARY.]

What do you want?

APOTH.— Thank heaven, I have found her!
My sweet! my soul! my own! my life's elixir!

NURSE— Blessed if it ain't that dratted old pill mixer!
Parson, do you admit such characters as them?

APOTH.—Ain't I a *piller* of the church?—*Ahem!*

FR. LA.—Peace to this trifling! in this sanctuary
A pun is instant death, therefore be wary!
But you are well arrived, for we are needing
A witness to a kind of—law proceeding—
Can you two keep a secret?

NURSE— I'm an oyster!

Aᴘᴏᴛʜ.—And I, as close as any first-class cloister.
Fʀ. Lᴀ.—Then let me tell you

[*Leads them forward.*]

I'm about to marry—
Nᴜʀsᴇ— What, you? and you a priest!
Aᴘᴏᴛʜ.— The ancient Harry!
Fʀ. Lᴀ.—No—no—I am about to marry two
Of your acquaintances.
Nᴜʀsᴇ— Why, bless me! Who?
Fʀ. Lᴀ.—Come forth, my friends!

[Rᴏᴍᴇᴏ *and* Jᴜʟɪᴇᴛ *come out.*]

These are the parties!
Nᴜʀsᴇ— Juliet!
Aᴘᴏᴛʜ.—The serenader! Hasn't he grown cool yet?
Nᴜʀsᴇ— You marry, and not tell your dear old nursey?
Fʀ. Lᴀ.—Yes—you're to be a witness.
Nᴜʀsᴇ— Me? Why, mercy!
I ain't dressed up!
Fʀ. Lᴀ.— I will not be denied!
You, sir, will have to give away the bride.
Aᴘᴏᴛʜ.—Give her away? Ask me to keep her secret,
And then give her away? Friar Laurence, I regret
I cannot do it! I'm not that kind of man!
Fʀ. Lᴀ.—Don't be an ass! I ask it, and you *can!*
You see that line? The nurse and you just toe it!
Now, holy brothers, are you ready?
Fʀs.— Go it!

Air—"Rᴜᴍ-sᴛʏ-ᴏʜ."

ɪ.

Fʀ. Lᴀ.— Do you each other's love endorse?
Aʟʟ— Yes they do, yes they do!
Fʀ. Lᴀ.— Without compunction or remorse?
Aʟʟ— Yes, etc.
Fʀ. Lᴀ.— Do you persist in this wild course?
Aʟʟ— Yes, etc.
Fʀ. Lᴀ.— Till parted by a square divorce?
Aʟʟ— Yes, etc.

II.

Fr. La.—	Do you two folks agree to wed?
All.—	Yes, etc.
Fr. La.—	To shut your eyes and go ahead?
All.—	Yes, etc.
Fr. La.—	To hang together like the old Ned?
	And hang until you're dead, dead, dead!
All.—	Yes, etc.
Rom.—	A very short affair, it seems to me—
	Is that all?
Fr. La.—	Yes, except the usual fee.
Rom.—	Well, chalk it up behind the chapel door.
Fr. La.—	We don't give tick on weddings any more.
Rom.—	You'll have to now, old fellow, we are tied;
	One thing you *can* do—you can kiss the bride!

[FRIAR LAURENCE *kisses* JULIET.]

Fr. La.—That's good! but not so good as cash. You'll see
All future weddings shall be C. O. D.

[*Knocking right and left.*]

What, more intruders?

Jul.— Hide us, pious friar!

Fr. La.—You know the only hiding place—retire!

[ROMEO, JULIET, *and* OTHERS, *hide behind* FRIARS.]

Pull in your dress, it's still in sight, my dear—
Enter, whoever knocks.

[*Enter* TYBALT *and* MERCUTIO *right and left.*]

Merc.— Is Romeo here?

Rom. [*to Friar*]—Say no.

Tyb.— Where is my cousin Juliet?

Jul. [*to Friar*]— Say don't know!

Fr. La.— Gentlemen, you both forget
I have retired from life, and cannot know
How the world's votaries may come and go—
In quiet prayer I pass—

Tyb.— Oh, hang your prayer,
I pass it, too. I've just been made aware
That Juliet, with that villain Romeo—

Merc.— He is my kinsman, I would have you know!

TYB.— A villain all the same—and you're another!

MERC.— I'd fight you just as lief as not!

TYB.— I'd ruther!

FR. LA.—Peace, gentlemen—remember where you are!

ROM.— Don't let 'em!

JUL.— Stop 'em!

NURSE— Watch!

APOTH.— St' boy!

FRS.— Beware!

Air—" GENS D'ARMES DUET."

MERC. [*draws*]— Now, rascal, thy passado!

TYB. [*draws*]— Have at thee, king of cats!

FR. LA.— Oh, cease this wild bravado!

JUL. [*pops out*]— Why will they have such spats!

APOTH. [*pops out*]—Pitch in! you'll need a surgeon!

NURSE— Their rage you oughtn't urge on!

FR. LA.— Stop the fight!

ALL— Stop the fight!

FR. LA.— Stop the fight!

ALL.— Stop the fight!

A murder will this verge on!

MERC.— I am dead!

ALL— He is dead!

MERC.— I am dead!

ALL— He is dead!

A murder's committed!

ROM. [*springs out*]— You wretch, you've killed my kinsman!

TYB.— And I can kill you, too!

APOTH. [*comes out*]—Stand steady on your pins, man!

JUL. [*comes out*]— Oh, this is sad to view!

NURSE— I don't know which to back up!

FR. LA.— Their carcasses they'll hack up!

Stop the fight!

ALL— Stop the fight.

FR. LA.— Stop the fight.

ALL— Stop the fight

Another life they'll whack up.

TYB.— I am dead.

ALL— He is dead.

TYB.— I am dead.

ALL— He is dead,

Another life is sped.

— 34 —

JUL.—   Ah, love, too long in this fell place we've tarried,
         First mine, and then my cousin's beauty you have
APOTH. [*feels Mercutio*]—   [mar-red.
         No pulse! no breath! he's deader than a ducat.
NURSE [*over Tybalt*]—
         He's very dead, and here's were he was stuck at!
FR. LA.—Well, Romeo, this is something of a scrape!
ROM.—   You're right it is! and how shall I escape?

Air—"JOHNNY COMES MARCHING HOME."

FR. LA.—What do you think he'd better do?
ALL—   Better get up and get!
FR. LA.—Isn't there any way out of the stew?
ALL—   Better get up and get!
FR. LA.—Couldn't he keep around and about?
         Hold up his head and brazen it out?
ALL—   He might do so, but we doubt—
         Better get up and get!

FR. LA.—Couldn't we put in an alibi?
ALL—   Better get up and get!
FR. LA.—Couldn't he one or two jurymen buy?
ALL—   Better get up and get!
FR. LA.—Don't you believe we could put in a plea
         Of emotional insanity?
ALL—   That lacks novelty,
         Better get up and get!

FR. LA.—Couldn't he get a judge on his side?
ALL—   Better get up and get!
FR. LA.—How's justifiable homicide?
ALL—   Better get up and get!
FR. LA.—We could cook up a deal of evidence
         To prove it a case of self-defence!
ALL—   Lawyer's fees are a great expense!
         Better get up and get.

FR. LA.—I fear that they are right, good Romeo!
         So osculate poor Mrs. R., and go!
ROM.—   I'll start upon a hurried foreign mission,
         To some place out of reach of extradition!
         Farewell, 'tis but a little while, my honey!
JUL.—   My husband! (*sobs*) can't you leave me any money!
ROM.—   Draw on me thro' the bank at Mantua.

Good-bye!
FR. LA.—   Be gone, sir!
ROM.—   I bego!
JUL.—   Ta, ta!

[*Exit* ROMEO.]

Poor Tybalt! prematurely gone to glory!
FR. LA.—I mourn Mercutio, lachrymarum rore.

Air.—"MASSA'S IN THE COLD, COLD GROUND."

JUL.—   Both were elegantly tall, sirs!
            Most devoted of our beaux.
            They were two such lovely waltzers—
            All the girls will mourn their close.

CHO.—   All of Verona's
            Belles will mourn their fates,
            They will miss such willing escorts,
            And such fluent tête-à-têtes.

FR. LA.—Juliet! a sudden consolation stirs me!
            Tybalt, the late deceased, unless it errs me,
            Was only son.
JUL.—   He was!
FR. LA.—   He being dead,
            You have his property inherited!
JUL.—   That's so!
FR. LA.—   Allow me a respectful caress,
            You are, dear Madam R., a bloated heiress!

Air—"YANKEE DOODLE."

JUL.—   Yes, that's so, I'm rich as a Croe-
            Sus ever was, or Dido;
            A happy girl I ought to be,
            An heiress and a bride, oh!

CHORUS AND DANCE.—
            Now's the time to dance and sing,
            What care we for dead men!
            Cash in hand's the only thing
            To make us honor-ed men.

                        [*Repeat.*]
       [*Curtain.*]

SCENE V.

[*Street in Verona. Chorus of* APPRENTICES *to the* APOTHECARY.]
Air—"DIXIE"

I.

SOLO— I am the druggist's new apprentice,
For mixing pills and squills my bent is.
CHO.— I'm a gay, I'm a gay, I'm a gay apothecary.
SOLO— I am the lad who draws the soda
With aromatic smile and odor.
CHO.— I'm a gay, I'm a gay, I'm a gay apothecary.
For calomel and senna, hurrah! hurrah!
For ipecacuanha, boys,
We'll raise a loud hosannah.
I want—to be—a first-class pharmaceutist,
- I want—to be—a first-class pharmaceutist.

II.

SOLO— You want a medicine for coughin'?
I'll fix you up a dose of morphine.
CHO.— I'm a gay, I'm a gay, I'm a gay apothecary.
SOLO— And if your baby has the colic,
In laudanum I'll let it rollick.
CHO.— I'm a gay, I'm a gay, I'm a gay apothecary.
For calomel and senna, hurrah! hurrah! etc.

[*Enter* APOTHECARY.]

APOTH.—Young men, why fritter thus your time away?
When tempting tinctures wait, and balsams gay.
The stolid lad I would not give a flam for,
Who feels no joy in chamomile or camphor!
In natures admirably constituted
The spirit pants for quinine undiluted.
Back to your labors! diligently wrestle
With spatula and minim, scale and pestle.
Yet while the salts you mash and acids slop,
Be sure to keep an eye upon the shop.

[*Exeunt* APPRENTICES.]

Now will I to my inmost den retire,
Where all sweet odors poesy inspire.
This madly seething brain will I immerse
In scribbling sonnets to my charming nurse.

[*Exit* APOTHECARY.]

Air—" DRINKING SONG," *from* GIROFLE.

CHO. [*within*]—

I.

Reach me, my crony, a drachm of ammonia
Carefully cull four scruples of sulphur,
Pound at it louder—pound it to powder,
Moisten it well with cod liver oil !

II.

Sarsaparilla does'nt go ill a-
Long with potassia—wormwood and cassia,
Iodine's really a—kin to lobelia,
All together will mix for a dose.

III.

Make it more placid, stir in an acid,
When it is wetted—ah ! add assafœtida,
Then you will see a pharmacopœia
All mixed up in one powerful pill.

[*Enter* ROMEO, *disguised in red whiskers and green goggles.*]

ROM.—   I'm here, and so far safe.   Even Juliet's eyes
Could not detect me under this disguise.
I wonder what has happened since my row,
And what the coroner said, and where's my frau ;
I see no newsboys, but perhaps I can
Find a Verona Globe-Republican
At this apothecary's.   Ho, within !
What ho !
APOTH. [*within*]—   Who raises such unnecessary din ?
We have no hoe within, young man, this 'ere house
Is not an agricultural tool warehouse !

[*Withdraws.*]

Rom.— Have you a morning paper? He is gone—
Who comes? 'tis Juliet's nurse! she looks forlorn.
Hullo! young woman!

Nurse— Don't be quite so free!
Why, *all* the men are making up to me!

Rom.— But don't you know me?

Nurse— Know you! no! not I!
I wouldn't know so hideous a guy—
An odious red-haired Irishman. Good-bye!

Rom.— Stop but a moment, beautiful young peri—
I am a stranger; I would put a query;

Nurse— The gentleman's politer than he's pretty--
Well, sir, what is it?

Rom.— I don't know your city,
And want to find a friend. Can you tell where
One Capulet lives?

Nusre— Which Capulet?

Rom.— The mayor!
He has a daughter Juliet!

Nurse— He *had* her;
Alas, poor thing! no death could e'er be sadder!

Rom.— Who's dead?

Nurse— Juliet, the child of my affection.
In taking arsenic for her complexion,
She took too much, and now in heaven she's sainted.
I laid her out—

[Romeo *shrieks and falls.*]

My stars! the man has fainted

[*Enter* Apothecary *and* Apprentices.]

Air.—" Co-ca-che-lunk.."

Nurse— Oh! Mr. Man, this fellow has fainted;
He has gone off in a kind of a fit,
It is a stroke of paralysis, ain't it?
Perhaps he has gone to the bottomless pit!

Cho.— Dose him with creosote, fill him with bromine,
Rub his temples with alum and myrrh;
Give him a pailful of cannabis Indica;
Croton oil his eyes will stir.

NURSE— Give me a sponge to bathe his forehead;
Give me a feather to tickle his nose;
Give me a— [*to* APOTHECARY.]
Sir, your conduct is horrid!—
Mustard poultice to tie to his toes.
CHO.— Dose him with creosote, etc.

APOTH.—He's still unconscious—lovely angel, hear me; [me!
NURSE— Shut up your mouth; and don't you come so near
He's breathing yet;
APOTH.— Yes, mum, he's not quite dead.
Oh, do not say that all my hopes are fled!
NURSE— Oh, drat the man! can't you hold up a minute?
He groans;
APOTH.— He'll soon be chipper as a linnet.
My dearest little duckey!
NURSE— Oh, I wish you
Would quit! His eyes are open!
APOTH.— Let me kiss you?
NURSE— Confound you, if you can't behave, I'll go!
APOTH.—Stay, I beseech you! I'll do better!
NURSE— No!
[*Exit.*]
ROM. [*sits up*]—
Good friends, have you no medicine for woe?
APOTH.—Of course we have, a wonderful specific.
If you will take it, you'll feel beatific.
ROM.— What is it?
APOTH.— Boys, his question do you hear?
Tell him about our famous panacea!

Air—"BEAUTIFUL STAR."

SOLO— Rhubarb and tar is bound to be
The universal remedy;
Children all cry for it—so does their ma.
Cure for all sicknesses—rhubarb and tar;
Cure for all sicknesses—rhubarb and tar.
CHO.— Rhubarb and tar, rhubarb and tar; [tar.
Cure for all sicknesses—rhubarb, red rhubarb and
ROM.— I want no kind of patent-medicine medley;
I want a poison, swift, and sure, and deadly!
APOTH.—We cannot sell you poison, sir, unless
Prescribed by some doctor or doctoress.

Rom.— I want a dose to kill a brood of rats
That haunt my premises.
Apoth.—   Oh, well, if that's
The case, I'll sell ten grains of arsenic
For six bits—that will kill them mighty quick.
Rom.— For six bits! Too much; I'll only give you four.
The usual druggist's profits I will give—
Ten times the cost, but not a nickel more!
Apoth.—Great goodness, man! how do you think we live?
This arsenic costs millions to prepare.
I ought to charge much higher, 'tis so rare;
I sell it thus for charity.
Rom.—   Oh, quits!
I'll give you not a cent beyond four bits.
Apoth.—Well, take it! but take also my advice:
When you buy drugs, don't higgle at the price.
Rom.— I will, I will—ahem!

[*Whispers to his neighbor, "Prompt me."* Apothecary—*"Prompt him."*
All whisper, " Prompt him."]

Air—"Shool, Shool."

Rom.— Now, Mr. Prompter, don't get vexed,
I've studied hard to learn the text,
But disremember what comes next;
Whisper loud and give the cue!
Cho.— Shoo, shoo! you've lost your cue,
Go to the prompter and start anew;
And when you get another start,
Don't try again 'til you know your part.

[*Repeat.*]

Prom.— I'll take this potent poison and skedaddle,
All [*to* Rom.]—
I'll take this potent poison and skedaddle,
Rom.— I'll take this potent poison and skedaddle
Across the Styx, my own canoe to paddle.
Juliet is dead, the lady that I tie to;
There's nothing left for me to do but die, too.
Farewell, good gentlemen, your arsenic
Will make me—no, my rats—uncommon sick.

Air—"MAID OF ATHENS."

Rom.— Gentle druggists, ere I start,
Thanks I give with all my heart,
For your aid in my distress ;
Sirs, I wish you all success.

Cho.— Gentle stranger, ere you go,
Pay, oh, pay the sum you owe ;
To escape the sheriff's writs,
Pay us fifty cents—four bits.

Rom.— Beg your pardon, I forgot,
In my right mind I am not ;
Here's the change to pay my scot,
Take the stamps and let me trot.

Cho.— Gentle stranger, we are square,
You may to your rats repair.
These four bits have rung their knell ;
Gentle stranger, fare thee well.

[*Curtain.*]

SCENE VI.

[A cemetery; large tomb in the center, flanked by two fresh tombstones. Inscriptions :

IN MEMORY OF

JULIET,

ONLY CHILD OF

EBENEZER H. AND LULU CAPULET.

Born Aug. 4, 1833; Died Jan. 16, 1877.

AGED 14.

HIC JACET	HERE LIES THE BODY OF
DANIEL WEBSTER MERCUTIO.	H. CLAY TYBALT CAPULET.
	SLAIN IN BATTLE,
Obit Jan. 13, 1877.	*Jan. 13, 1877.*

Enter procession of FRIARS, *carrying* JULIET *on a bier, followed by* NURSE.]

Air—"HOME BY THE SEA."

I.

CHO.—   We come through the gathering gloom,
To bury our sweetest and best;
We come to the Capulet's tomb,
To lay our young darling to rest.
We mourn for the fair Juliet;
We mourn for her, silent and dead.
Go slow, she is making us sweat.
Go slow, she is as heavy as lead.
Go slow, go slow, go slow, she is heavy as lead!
Go slow, go slow, go slow, she is heavy as lead!

II.

We're glad that the trip is so short—
That the kirkyard's so near to the kirk;
These funeral lifts are no sport,
But the gravest description of work,

We've come to the family lot,
Yes this is her monument here;
Set the bier down, and come get a pot
Of another variety of beer.
Let us go, let us go, let us go get a glass of good beer;
Let us go, let us go, let us go get a glass of good beer.

[*Exeunt* FRIARS.]

NURSE— Well, this is nice! alone in such a place,
With two fresh tombstones staring in my face!
I'm scared; I shouldn't dare to look across 'em,
Unless I knew that Jule was playing 'possum!
Poor child! they wanted her to marry Paris.
She doesn't care how many men she marries,
But wants one husband fairly dead and buried,
And his insurance to her credit kerried
Before she takes another. Her old daddy
Swore she should wed to-day the other laddie;   ✓
So to gain time to hear from Romeo,
Whose post-office address she didn't know,
I bought a sleeping powder, which she took it,
And I gave out as how she kicked the bucket;
—I hope the Friar will hurry up—'twould be
A little awkward if the crowd should see,
Right in the middle of a powerful prayer,
The corpse sit up and rub her eyes and stare!
Bless me! I'm tired: I'll just sit down and wait,
Folks come to funerals, like parties—late.

[*Sits down and dozes.*]

[*Enter* ROMEO.]

ROM.— To be or not to be—oh, I forget,
I'm playing Romeo, not Ham-u-let.
About this time Paris I ought to slay,
But can't, because he's not cast in our play.
This is the place; yonder the the tomb—ah me!
It is my love's sweet, silent self I see!
Oh, Juliet! my wife! I have consulted
Good lawyers as to how thy death resulted.
They tell me that, so far as they can ferret
The law out, I cannot your wealth inherit;
And so of thee and fortune both bereft,

A pauper relict I will not be left.
Thou loveliest girl I ever set my eyes on,
One kiss, and then I'll get outside this pizon.

[*Drinks.*]

Juliet, here's hoping! True apothecary,
Thy drugs are quick ; on this soft spot I'll die.

[*Lies down and stretches out with a groan, which arouses the* NURSE, *who comes forward.*]

NURSE—· I'm mighty good so wide awake to keep ;
Most other persons would have gone to sleep
A sitting here so long. Mercy! what's that ?
A man? It's Romeo, all sprawled out flat ;
He's dead, poor boy ; a case of suicide ;
This little bottle shows just how he died.
Oh, this will be a fearful blow to her,
But 'tis a god-send to the coroner.

[*Enter* CAPULET, FRIAR LAURENCE, *and* CITIZENS, *in crape.*]

CAP.— What's this? another corpse?
NURSE— Your honor [*sob*],
'Tis Romeo! [*sob*] pizen! [*sob*] suicide! [*sob*] a
[goner !

Air—"UPIDEE."

FR. LA.— Oh, what a dreadful jamboree.
ALL— Very sad, very sad.
FR. LA.— It is a regular massacre.
ALL— Very sad indeed.
FR. LA.— 'Tis bad enough to bury one :
Another don't increase the fun.
CHO.— This kind of thing is very sad, very sad, very sad,
This kind of thing is very sad,
Very sad indeed.

[*Handkerchiefs out, noses blown rythmically six beats.*]

Oh! oh! oh!
This kind of thing is very sad, very sad, very sad,
This kind of thing is very sad,
Very sad indeed.

FR. LA.—It may be economical
ALL— Very sad, very sad,
FR. LA.—To give them both one funeral ;
ALL— Very sad indeed ;

Fr. La.—But either way I fear it will
    Augment the undertaker's bill.
All—   This kind of thing is very sad, etc.
Cap.—   But tell me, nurse, how came young Romeo here,
    And what has thrown the man so out of gear?
Nurse— The melancholy story you shall hear.
    Excuse me if I intersperse a tear!

Air—"Gaudeamus."

Nurse— This young lady and this young gent
      Loved each other clandestinely;
    They didn't think you would consent,
      'Cause their politics didn't agree;
    And as their love just gushed in torrents,
    They went and got the Reverend Laurence
      To marry them immediately.
All—   To marry them immediately.
Nurse—   Before they had a chance to go,
    The chaps who own those tombstones grim,
      Came in and had an awful row,
    One killed the other, then he killed him,
      So out he lit, but ventured back
      And rashly took an arsenic snack,
    'Cause his wife had doused her glim.
All—   'Cause his wife had doused her glim.
Nurse— I would explain "had doused her glim" to be
    A nautical expression, used at sea—
    It means, had died.
Cap.—   Yes, we knew that before.   [more.
Nurse— You did? Then perhaps you'd like to know some
    She hasn't doused her glim!
Cap.—   What's that you said?
Nurse— I said she isn't dead!
All—   She isn't dead?
Nurse— You hear me? No she's no more dead than we are!
Fr. [*aside*]—She's weak about the occiput, I fear!
Cap.—   What mean you? Set at rest the wild anxiety
    This fond heart feels. Speak, woman!
Nurse—   I deny it I
    Am not a woman!
Cap.—   Tell me what you mean, eh!
    Or I will strangle you—á la Salvini!

NURSE— Please don't!

CAP.—   Then speak !

NURSE—   Well ! this poor young lady
Obliged to keep her marriage sort o' shady,
Was quite embarrassed when you tried to crowd her
To marry Paris, so she took a powder
That sent her off to sleep.

CAP.—   This is confusing.
Then she's not dead ?

NURSE—   Lud, no, she's only snoozing.

CAP.— The little rascal ! only playing Quaker ;
Come up, my friends, and help me try and wake her.

Air—"MARYLAND."

I wouldn't have you think me gruff,
 But wake at once, my daughter;
Your nap has lasted long enough,
 Rouse up. You really ought ter.

ALL— To wake her up, to wake her up,
 Your way's too soporific;
Let us unite with all our might,
 And give a yell terrific:
         Whoop!

JUL. [*stirs*]— Oh, let me be! Oh, let me be!
 I thought I gave you warning—
Society girls you never see
 At breakfast in the morning.

ALL—   To wake her up, etc.
         Whoop!

JUL. [*sits up*]—Where am I, and who am I?

CAP.—   I'm upset
By all this, but I think you're Juliet.

FR.— And I would add that you're the principal
Performer at a first-class funeral.

JUL.— Methinks you married me awhile ago !

FR.— I'm sorry for it, Mrs. Romeo !

JUL.— Why sorry ?

FR.—   Pardon the tear that copious flows
Your husband up to heaven has turned his toes.
Behold him !

JUL.—   Romeo ! intoxicated?

CAP.— No, Jule, on arsenic he dissipated
An " A 1 " widow you may now be rated !

JUL.—   Ah, woe is me! my husband!
CAP.—   What a job!
FR. LA.—Suppose we fetch a sympathetic sob!

[*Enter* APOTHECARY.]

APOTH.—What's all this coil ?
NURSE—   This gentleman has fed
On too much arsenic, and he's dead.
APOTH.—How long ago ?
CAP.—   Not fifteen minutes.
APOTH.—   Then
He might perchance be brought to life again.
JUL.—   How say you ?
NURSE—   Oh, return him quick to life!
APOTH.—I will, if you'll consent to be my wife!
JUL.—   Of course you will, won't you sweet nurse ?
NURSE—   Oh, yes !
(*Aside*) This is a promise given under duress.
APOTH.—I'll get my instrument.
FRIAR—   I'll help ; is't bulky ?
APOTH.—Oh, no, I have it right here, in my sulky.

[*Exit* APOTHECARY.]

Air—"RED, WHITE AND BLUE."

JUL.—   Oh, fly on the wings of the breezes,
          And fetch in your tools on the jump,
        My heart with anxiety freezes,
          And hangs in my throat like a lump.

[*Re-enter* APOTHECARY *with garden squirt.*]

ALL—   He is here with his little stomach pump.
        He is here with his little stomach pump.
        He can bring him to life, if he pleases,
        With the aid of his little stomach pump.
JUL.—   Success has attended your mission,
          And now all your skill you must hump ;
        Set up your machine in position,
          And do not let it slip up or slump.
ALL—   He is here with his little stomach pump,
        He is here with his little stomach pump,
        Behold what this noble physician
        Will do with his little stomach pump.
JUL.—   Hist, while he works! disturb him not!
APOTH.—   Oh, sho!

Is this the fellow they call Romeo?
JUL.—   'Tis he!
ALL—   'Tis he!
APOTH.—   Then he don't need my aid.
JUL.—   Why so?
ALL—   Why so?
APOTH.—   Because, when I purveyed
The arsenic he wanted " to kill mice,"
He tried to beat me down below my price;
At last, after a deal of fuss and talk,
I took his money, but I sold him—chalk!
JUL.—   Then he's not poisoned?
APOTH.—   Not materially.
Just stir him up, my dear, and you will see.
JUL.—   Romeo, arouse thee!
ROM.—   Yes'm. I arise.
FRIAR—   A miracle!
CAP.—   Bad penny!
NURSE—   Bless my eyes!
JUL.—   To celebrate this wonderful awaking,
Good friends, let us indulge in merry-making!

[TYBALT *and* MERCUTIO *sit up behind their tombstones.*]

Air—"ADIEU! ADIEU!"

TYB. *and* MERC.—
Hold on, hold on, good friends, hold on a little bit!
For we respectfully submit
That if you think we're going to lie here dead,
You're very apt to be misled.
ALL—   Yes; that's to be expected.
If we'd had you both dissected,
You would still have resurrected,
              Out of spite.
Oh! well; there 'pears to be, whatever we may do,
No way of getting rid of you;
And since you seem not dead enough to hurt,
Crawl out, and shovel back the dirt!
MERC.—   I should have said,—my tardy memory rouses,—
When I was killed, " a plague o' both your houses."
JUL.—   Don't say it now, a plague to us returned
When your and Tybalt's ashes were un-urned!
My Romeo, happily resuscitated.

We were so quickly wed and separated,
Our nuptial morn did not the chance allow—
Suppose we have a swell reception now ?

APOTH.— And why should *we* not have a wedding, too ?
Sweet angel ! make thy recent promise true !

NURSE— You didn't resurrect him ! how you talk !

APOTH.—No, but I saved his precious life with chalk !

NURSE— Well, if you're so persistent, I suppose
There's no use in my following up my noes—
So here's my hand !

APOTH.—   And *now* I'll have that kiss !

ROM.—   A ditto, Juliet, would not come amiss.

Air—"LOUISIANA LOWLANDS."

NURSE—   Oh, no, I can't allow it
Before so many folks !
At least, I can't allow it
Unless you tease and coax.
And, then I am afraid
That one would not suffice—
Well, you may take one little one—
My ! warn't it awful nice ?

ALL—   And we'll marry them in Verona, Verona, Verona !
And we'll marry them in Verona, oh !

ROM.—   My dear little wife,
As we've all come to life,
And both of our ladies are married.
Our friends here before us
Would join in a chorus
Of hisses and groans, if we tarried.

JUL.—   Yes, love; I propose
That we bring to a close
This play, of its tragedy shorn,
That so we may quell,
With a timely farewell,
Their plain inclination to yawn.

Air—"STAR-SPANGLED BANNER."

JUL.—   Well, what do you think,
Now our drama is done,
Of our novel rendition of Shakespeare's old story ?

The best we can claim
Is to stir up some fun
With our rollicking choruses sung *con amore*.
And while we essay
To be carelessly gay,
Unite in our motto to laugh while we may;
And grant us one round of applause as you go,
For the gentle Juliet and the rare Romeo!

ALL—   And grant us one round of applause as you go,
For the gentle Juliet and the rare Romeo!

Charles Soule

A new travesty on Romeo and Juliet
As presented before the University club of St. Louis, January 16, 1877

ISBN/EAN: 9783337210489

Printed in Europe, USA, Canada, Australia, Japan

Cover: Foto ©Andreas Hilbeck / pixelio.de

More available books at **www.hansebooks.com**